The Kingdom of Wrenly

8

The Secret World of Mermaids

By Jordan Quinn
Illustrated by Robert McPhillips

LITTLE SIMON

New York London Toronto Sydney New Delhi

LITTLE SIMON
An imprint of Simon & Schuster Children's Publishing Division
1230 Avenue of the Americas, New York, New York 10020
First Little Simon hardcover edition May 2015
Copyright © 2015 by Simon & Schuster, Inc.
Also available in a Little Simon paperback edition.
All rights reserved, including the right of reproduction in whole or in part in any form.
LITTLE SIMON is a registered trademark of Simon & Schuster, Inc., and associated colophon is a trademark of Simon & Schuster, Inc.
For information about special discounts for bulk purchases, please contact Simon & Schuster Special Sales at 1-866-506-1949 or business@simonandschuster.com.
The Simon & Schuster Speakers Bureau can bring authors to your live event. For more information or to book an event contact the Simon & Schuster Speakers Bureau at 1-866-248-3049 or visit our website at www.simonspeakers.com.
Manufactured in the United States of America 0415 FFG
2 4 6 8 10 9 7 5 3 1
Library of Congress Cataloging-in-Publication Data
Quinn, Jordan.
The secret world of mermaids / by Jordan Quinn ; illustrated by Robert McPhillips. — First Little Simon edition.
    pages cm. — (The kingdom of Wrenly ; 8)
Summary: Lucas and Clara are floating on a raft when a wave casts them into the sea, where Lucas catches a glimpse of a coral kindom and a dark-haired mermaid helps him, but when his father, King Caleb, hears of this, he scolds Lucas and tells him he has broken an age-old pact.
ISBN 978-1-4814-3122-4 (pbk : alk. paper) — ISBN 978-1-4814-3123-1 (hc : alk. paper) — ISBN 978-1-4814-3124-8 (ebook) [1. Mermaids—Fiction. 2. Friendship—Fiction. 3. Princes—Fiction. 4. Kings, queens, rulers, etc.—Fiction.] I. McPhillips, Robert, illustrator. II. Title.
PZ7.Q31945Sf 2015
[Fic]—dc23
2014036040

CONTENTS

CHAPTER 1

My Turn

Swish! Swish! Swish! Prince Lucas and his best friend, Clara, swept dirt, leaves, and bits of straw into a corner of Ruskin's lair. They wanted the cave to be clean and perfect when Ruskin returned. Ruskin was on the island of Crestwood for the week. He was perfecting his fire-breathing skills, and Grom, the wizard overseeing Ruskin's training,

had told Lucas that being around other dragons every once in a while was good for him.

"Look at all the cobwebs!" cried Clara, pointing to shadowy corners of the lair.

"This place looks more like a

home for spiders than for a dragon," said Lucas.

They turned their brooms upside down and began to brush the webs from the corners of the lair. Spiders scurried into the cracks between the stones.

"I can't wait until Ruskin can go on more adventures with us," Lucas said.

"Me too," agreed Clara. "I wonder what land we'll discover next."

"Well, wherever it is," answered Lucas, "*I'm* going to be the one to discover it!"

Clara stopped sweeping the walls for a moment. "Why do you say it like *that*?" she asked.

Lucas shrugged. "I don't know. I guess it's because you always discover everything first," he said.

"I'm not trying to," responded Clara. "It's just because I know my way around the kingdom from all the bread deliveries I've done with my father."

"I know," said Lucas, "but I wish I could discover something before you just once."

Clara pulled a cobweb from her sleeve. "You're being silly," she said. "Besides, we've discovered lots of things *together*."

"Like what?" questioned Lucas.

Clara thought for a moment. "How about the time we found the Breach in the Starless Forest—

remember?" she said. "We collected the healing vixberries for Ruskin!"

Lucas shook his head. "But don't forget it was *your* friend who showed us the Breach," he protested. "I would never have discovered it if it weren't for you!"

"Why does that matter?" asked Clara.

"Because we never would have found the Breach and saved Ruskin's life if you hadn't been friends with Bren."

Clara rested her broom against the wall. She didn't want her best friend to be upset with her, even if it was for a silly reason.

"Well, don't worry," she said,

pulling off a cobweb. "I know you'll
uncover many mysteries before me.
Just keep your eyes open."

Lucas nodded. "You bet I will," he
said.

CHAPTER 2

The Raft

"What do you want to do today?" asked Clara as the two friends met on the palace steps.

"Discover a new land," said Lucas.

Clara rolled her eyes.

"Besides that," she said.

Lucas looked toward the water. "Want to build a sand castle?" he suggested.

Clara smiled. "Now, that's more

like it!" she said.

Lucas and Clara walked to Mermaid's Cove and worked on a sand castle all morning.

The tide had nearly reached the castle. Lucas dug a path from the moat to the edge of the water.

Seawater quickly began to fill the moat. Lucas plopped two hermit crabs onto the drawbridge.

"The hermit crabs will protect the sand castle from enemies," said Lucas.

"Good idea," said Clara as she stuck a sand dollar above the castle entrance. "What shall we call our castle?" she asked.

Lucas looked at their creation. The sand sparkled in the sun. The hermit crabs scuttled toward the moat. Small pieces of coral stood around the castle like leafless trees.

"How about Coral Castle?" he suggested.

Clara smiled and brushed loose strands of hair from her face with the back of her hand. "That's perfect," she said. She began to roll up

her pants. "Now let's go cool off."

"Right behind you!" said Lucas.

The waves rolled over their feet as
they walked along the water. Then
Lucas noticed something sticking
out of some seaweed farther down
the shore.

"What's that?" he said, pointing at the tangled green mess.

The children ran down the beach to see what the sea had washed up.

"It's a raft!" exclaimed Lucas.

They freed the raft from the sea-weed. It was made from several rows of narrow logs tied together with ropes.

"It looks pretty strong," said Lucas. "Let's take it out!"

Clara looked at the water. "We'd better not," she said. "The waves look kind of big."

"We can handle it," said Lucas. "Besides, it'll be so much fun!"

"What will we use for paddles?" asked Clara.

"I'll find some!" Lucas said.

Then he raced to another pile of seaweed and poked around. He quickly came back with two long pieces of driftwood and laid them on top of the raft.

"Ready to cast off!" he cried, dragging the

raft into the shallow water.

The raft bobbed up and down in the waves. Clara picked up one of the pieces of driftwood and carefully climbed on board.

"I'm not sure about this," she mumbled.

CHAPTER 3

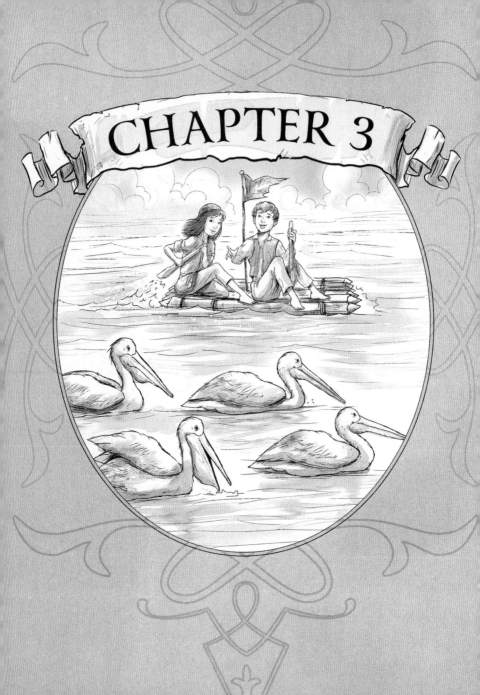

Man Overboard

Lucas and Clara sat on the raft and paddled away from Mermaid's Cove. They passed a line of pelicans fishing in the water. Playful waves splashed against the sides of the raft. Lucas yanked a clump of seaweed from between the logs and tossed it into the water. Then he continued paddling.

This raft sure feels nice and sturdy,

he thought. *And these driftwood paddles are perfect too.* He looked out to sea and smiled proudly. He hadn't discovered a new land or anything, but at least he and his best friend were out having a fun adventure anyway.

24

Beyond the reef, the waves began to get bigger. Seawater sloshed over the sides of the raft and soaked their clothes. The farther out they went, the bigger the waves got. The little raft bobbed up and down. The salt water splashed their faces.

They paddled over a coral
reef. Schools of colorful fish
swam beneath them. A seal
playfully poked his head above
the water and quickly disappeared
back under. Lucas and Clara
giggled.

"I think we should turn around!" Clara shouted over the wind and waves.

But Lucas didn't hear his friend's cry. Something else had caught his attention.

"Look up ahead!" he shouted,
pointing with his paddle. "A pod of
dolphins!"

Clara stopped paddling, and
together, they watched the dolphins
leap high into the air and dive back
into the water. *Splish! Splash!* The

dolphin show lasted several minutes. Neither of the children noticed as the wind blew the raft farther out to sea.

Clara looked back at the beach. It had gotten very far away.

"Lucas, we need to turn back

NOW!" Clara cried. "We've gone too far out, and the waves are getting rough."

This time Lucas paid attention to his friend.

"You're right!" he called back. "If

we paddle on the same side, we'll be able to turn around."

Lucas and Clara paddled as hard as they could, but the raft barely turned at all.

"It's not working!" cried Clara.

"Keep paddling!" Lucas shouted.

They got up on their knees so they could paddle harder. The waves pushed against the raft. It rocked this way and that. Then a very large wave made the children lose their balance. They tumbled into the water. Clara quickly grabbed the side of the raft with both hands and climbed back on. Then she looked for her friend, but she didn't see him.

"Lucas?" she called. "Lucas!"

She watched the paddles drift

away on the waves. "LUCAS!" she
yelled. "WHERE ARE YOU?"

CHAPTER 4

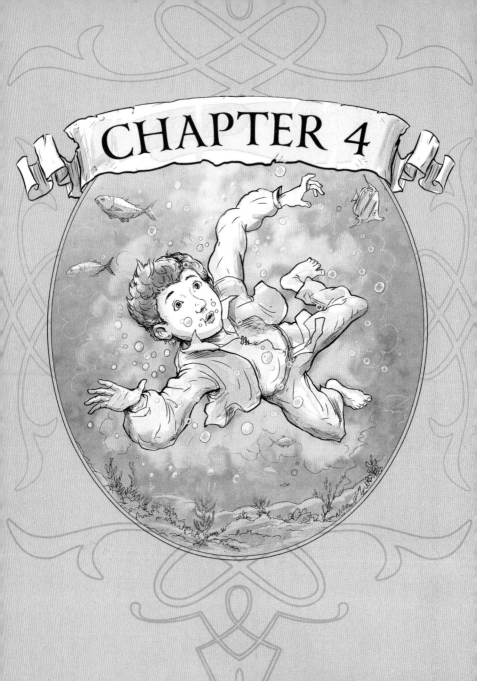

Under the Sea

Lucas plunged deep into the sea. The water bubbled past him as he sank below the surface. Down and down he went. He opened his eyes as he fell, and what he saw was enchanting. There, on the ocean floor, stood a magical kingdom made of shimmering coral.

I must be dreaming, he thought.

He stared at the glittering towers,

arches, and bridges beneath him. He noticed a young mermaid with long, flowing black hair peeking out from behind one of the windows.

His mouth dropped open. *This must be the kingdom of the mermaids!* he exclaimed to himself. The mermaid girl smiled at him. Lucas tried to smile back, but he needed to get to the surface—and fast. He was running out of air!

He spied the bottom of the raft and began to swim toward it. It suddenly looked very far

away. Then he felt something grab his arm. And there, next to him, was the mermaid girl from the window. She flicked her tail and swam Lucas back to the world above. As soon as his head broke the surface, he heard Clara's cries.

"Lucas!" shouted Clara when she saw her friend.

Lucas grabbed hold of the raft. His clothes felt heavy as he pulled himself on board.

"Oh, thank goodness!" she cried. "Are you okay?"

"I think so," Lucas said, gasping for breath.

Then he looked toward the shore. Mermaid's Cove was almost completely out of sight.

"We need to get back before we lose sight of the mainland," he said. "Let's lie down on our stomachs and paddle with our hands."

They both lay down and paddled
like sea turtles. The little raft began
to move forward. Then it began to
pick up speed.

"We're moving faster than we're
paddling!" shouted Clara.

"Something must be pushing us!"
Lucas shouted back.

"Maybe it's a dolphin!" Clara said.

"Maybe," said Lucas. *Or a mermaid,* he thought.

The raft slowed down as they approached the beach. Lucas looked over his shoulder. He thought he saw a mermaid tail flash in the sun and then disappear underwater.

The children jumped off the raft and walked the rest of the way to shore. Then they plopped down onto the wet sand to catch their breath.

CHAPTER 5

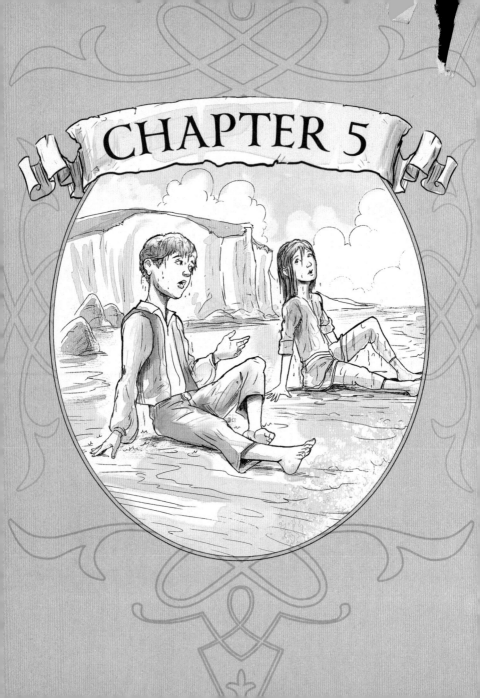

A Fishy Tale

"Are you okay?" Clara asked again as she propped herself up.

Lucas nodded. "I'm sorry, Clara," he said. "I should have listened to you."

"That's okay," said his friend, squinting at the sun. "But you had me terrified!" she went on. "It felt like you were underwater forever."

Lucas wrung some seawater

from his wet shirt. "Really? I wish I could have stayed longer." He sighed. "You're never going to believe what I saw down there," he said.

Clara's eyes grew wide. "What do you mean?" she asked. She leaned over excitedly.

"I saw something amazing and magical," he said. "I saw the Mermaid Kingdom!"

Clara's jaw dropped. "But that's

impossible!" she declared. "Everyone says that the Mermaid Kingdom is hidden from human sight."

"I know!" agreed Lucas. "But I'm telling you, I *saw* it! And it was the most incredible thing I've ever seen."

Then he tried to describe the sparkling coral kingdom and the mermaid girl who had rescued him.

"I think she helped us

get back to shore too," Lucas added.

Clara shook her head in disbelief. "But I sit here in Mermaid's Cove more than anyone else and *I've* never even seen a mermaid. Not even the tip of a tail!" she said. "Are you sure you're not making this up?"

"Why would I do that?" asked Lucas.

"Well, I don't know," Clara went on. "Maybe because you wanted so badly to discover something first. It's just hard to believe that you happened to find an *entire kingdom* the very next day. . . ."

"I see your point," said Lucas, "but I promise I'm *not* making this up."

Clara watched the waves crash and foam on the shore.

"Well, all I can say is that I'm really glad you're safe," she said.

Lucas smiled at his friend and

sighed. He was too tired to try to convince her anymore today.

"I'm really glad we're *both* safe," he said.

And he left it at that.

CHAPTER 6

An Ancient Pact

Lucas walked Clara home and then headed for the palace. He snuck in through the kitchen only to find his father, King Caleb, grabbing an apple from the fruit bowl.

The king glanced over at his son. Lucas's clothes were still dripping wet, and there were bits of sand on his face.

"Good heavens, boy! What have

you been up to now?" cried the king.

Lucas shrugged as if it were no big deal. "Clara and I went swimming at Mermaid's Cove," he answered.

"With all your clothes on?" questioned his father. Lucas wondered if he should tell the king what had happened. He didn't want to get in trouble, but he also wanted to ask his father about the

Mermaid Kingdom. He decided to tell the truth.

"Actually, we found a raft washed up on the beach," Lucas began. "And we paddled out into the cove."

The king raised an eyebrow.

"It was really fun," Lucas went on, "until the waves got too big . . .

and we kind of fell overboard."

"Kind of?" the king asked. "How do you *kind of* fall overboard?"

The prince shrugged. The king's

frown deepened.
Lucas knew what
was coming next.

"Lucas!" his
father bellowed.
"You are the heir
to the throne!
How could you
be so careless with
your safety?"

Lucas looked down
at his feet. "I'm very
sorry," he mumbled.

The king pointed out the window toward the distant water. "The

current is powerful," he went on. "You could have been swept out to sea!"

"I *promise* I'll be more careful from now on," Lucas said. Then he paused for a moment while his father calmed down. "But there's a little bit more. . . ."

The king's eyebrows rose and his brow wrinkled.

"Something strange happened when I was underwater."

"Go on," said the king.

So, Lucas told his father about how he had seen the kingdom of the

mermaids and how the mermaid girl
had helped him.

The king shook his head in disbelief. "Lucas, do you realize that the
mermaid broke an ancient pact to
help you?" he asked.

Lucas shook his head. He had
no idea what his father was talking
about.

"Long ago the mermaids made a

pact with the kingdom of Wrenly to keep out of sight of humans," said the king. "And in return we give them their privacy."

Lucas knew the mermaids never showed themselves, but he didn't know it was because of an ancient agreement with Wrenly. Either way, it didn't stop him from wanting to

find out more about the mermaids.

"Well, now that I've *seen* a mermaid," said Lucas, "may I go back and explore their kingdom?"

"Did you not hear what I just said?" questioned his father. "Our

promise is to honor the mermaids'
privacy. And the answer to your
question is *no*."

Lucas kicked the stone floor with
his wet boot.